How many Fairy Tales do you know?

How many questions can you answer?
It's fun to peek behind
the flap — to see if you
were right...

PRICE/STERN/SLOAN
Publishers, Inc., Los Angeles
1984

Who ate the Three Bears

porridge?

What did Jack find at the top of the beanstalk?

Who said "Grandma, what big eyes you've

got"?

What happened when Aladdin rubbed his lamp?

What did Puss wear on his feet?

Who lost a slipper
at the ball?

Whose house
was made of bricks?

How many dwarfs lived with Snow White?

Which little boy
was made
of wood?

Who did the prince wake up with a kiss?